Hello, Family Members,

Learning to read is one of the most important accomplishments of early childhood. **Hello Reader!** books are designed to help children become skilled readers who like to read. Beginning readers learn to read by remembering frequently used words like "the," "is," and "and"; by using phonics skills to decode new words; and by interpreting picture and text clues. These books provide both the stories children enjoy and the structure they need to read fluently and independently. Here are suggestions for helping your child *before*, *during*, and *after* reading:

Before

- Look at the cover and pictures and have your child predict what the story is about.
- Read the story to your child.
- Encourage your child to chime in with familiar words and phrases.
- Echo read with your child by reading a line first and having your child read it after you do.

During

- Have your child think about a word he or she does not recognize right away. Provide hints such as "Let's see if we know the sounds" and "Have we read other words like this one?"
- Encourage your child to use phonics skills to sound out new words.
- Provide the word for your child when more assistance is needed so that he or she does not struggle and the experience of reading with you is a positive one.
- Encourage your child to have fun by reading with a lot of expression . . . like an actor!

After

- Have your child keep lists of interesting and favorite words.
- Encourage your child to read the books over and over again. Have him or her read to brothers, sisters, grandparents, and even teddy bears. Repeated readings develop confidence in young readers.
- Talk about the stories. Ask and answer questions. Share ideas about the funniest and most interesting characters and events in the stories.

I do hope that you and your child enjoy this book.

—Francie Alexander
Reading Specialist,
Scholastic's Instructional Publishing Group

If you have questions or comments about how children learn to read, please contact Francie Alexander at FrancieAl@aol.com

To Kathleen Sullivan
—K.M.

To Steve,
who has spent hours posing
like a guinea pig
—M.S.

Library of Congress Cataloging-in-Publication Data
McMullan, Kate.
Fluffy's Valentine's Day/by Kate McMullan; illustrated by Mavis Smith.
p. cm.—(Hello reader! Level 3)
"Cartwheel books."
Summary: Fluffy endures a bath and shampoo at school on Valentine's Day, but when another guinea pig named Kiss is placed in his play yard, his patience snaps.
ISBN 0-590-37216-5
[1. Valentine's Day—Fiction. 2. Guinea pigs—Fiction. 3. Schools—Fiction.]
I. Smith, Mavis, ill. II. Title. III. Series.
PZ7.M2295F1 1997
[E]—dc21
97-15465
CIP
AC

10 9 8 7 6 9/9 0/0 01 02

Printed in the U.S.A. 24
First printing, January 1998

by Kate McMullan

Illustrated by Mavis Smith

Hello Reader!—Level 3

SCHOLASTIC INC.

New York Toronto London Auckland Sydney

Who Likes Valentine's Day?

"Tomorrow is Valentine's Day," said Ms. Day.
"Today we will make valentine boxes.
Decorate your box to show what you love."
They love ME! thought Fluffy.

FEBRUARY

The kids cut pictures out of magazines.
They pasted things on their boxes.
They sprinkled on glitter.
Nobody stopped by to see Fluffy
all morning.
I don't think I like Valentine's Day,
thought Fluffy.

Everyone worked hard until lunchtime.
No one checked to see
if Fluffy's food bowl was empty.
It wasn't.
But it could be, thought Fluffy.
And he burrowed under his straw.
I DON'T like Valentine's Day.

That afternoon, the kids shared their valentine boxes.
Fluffy peeked out at them from under the straw.

"I love pink," said Emma.

"I pasted pink ribbons on my box."

So what? thought Fluffy.

"I drew a heart on mine," Maxwell said.

Yawn, thought Fluffy.

"I pasted a picture of Yanda Blue on my box," said Jasmine. "She's the world's fastest woman."

Why not a picture of me? thought Fluffy. **The world's fastest guinea pig!**

"I love sharks," said Wade.
"That's what I drew on my box."
So go get a shark for class pet,
thought Fluffy.
I quit! Valentine's Day.
Bah! Who needs it?

Then Ms. Day said,
"Shall we show Fluffy his valentine box?"
Show me my WHAT? Fluffy thought.

67

"Surprise, Fluffy!" everyone shouted.

Jasmine and Wade held up a red box.

Black letters spelled out

WE LOVE YOU, FLUFFY!

You do? thought Fluffy.

Well, who can blame you?

I am one lovable pig.

Wade opened Fluffy's valentine box.
He took out a bright red apple.
Ms. Day cut it in half
and put it in Fluffy's cage.
Who likes Valentine's Day?
thought Fluffy. **I do!**

Fluffy Takes a Bath

Jasmine and Emma took Fluffy
for a walk in the hallway.
Their friend Lina came along.
When she saw Fluffy, Lina said,
"Awww, what's her name?"
His name, thought Fluffy.
I'm a boy pig.
But Jasmine only said, "Fluffy."
"She's so cute," said Lina.
"But she smells funny."
She does? Fluffy thought.
I mean, I do?

Fluffy gave himself a little sniff.
He had a fine guinea pig smell.
What was that silly girl talking about?

When they got back to the classroom,
Jasmine said, "Ms. Day, Fluffy needs a bath."
No way! thought Fluffy.
I do NOT need a bath!

"It'll make him smell good
for Valentine's Day," said Emma.
I smell good now! thought Fluffy.
I smell just right!
"That's a fine idea," said Ms. Day.
Hey! thought Fluffy.
Whose side are YOU on?

Emma put some warm water
in a plastic tub.
Jasmine started to lower Fluffy
into the water.
Stop! thought Fluffy.
He wiggled and kicked.
He squealed and squealed.
Help! Save me! Police!
Somebody! Anybody! Help!

"Fluffy!" said Emma.

"Stop acting like a baby!"

Who, me? thought Fluffy.

And Jasmine put him in the tub.

The warm bathwater
made Fluffy feel warm all over.
Okay, thought Fluffy.
I can handle this.

Emma squirted guinea pig shampoo
into her hand.

She rubbed it onto Fluffy's back.
The shampoo turned Fluffy
all white and foamy.
Look out! thought Fluffy.
I'm a big, bad polar bear!

Jasmine poured warm water over Fluffy
to rinse off the soap.
Now I'm a seal, thought Fluffy.
I'm swimming under
a waterfall!

Jasmine poured until the bubbles were gone.

Emma picked Fluffy up.

"Bath time's over," she said.

That's what you think! thought Fluffy.

He kicked and splashed.

He squealed and squealed.

You didn't wash my face!

What about my paws?

Hey! We're not finished here!

“What a fusser!” said Jasmine.
She dried Fluffy with a soft towel.
Then she took him over to a box.
Inside was a hot water bottle
wrapped in a towel.
Jasmine put Fluffy into the box.
“Stay here until you’re dry,” she said.

Fluffy stretched out on the towel.
He gave himself a little sniff.
He smelled like shampoo.
But under the shampoo,
he still had his fine guinea pig smell.
Maybe I'll need another bath tomorrow,
thought Fluffy.

A Kiss for Fluffy

Ms. Day's class invited Mr. Lee's class
to a Valentine's Day party.
Mr. Lee's class brought cupcakes,
candy hearts, and a guinea pig named Kiss.

Emma put Fluffy into his play yard.
Jemal from Mr. Lee's class put in Kiss.
"Maybe they'll fall in love," said Emma.
"Yuck," said Jemal.

Who are you? asked Fluffy.

I'm Kiss, said Kiss. **Who are you?**

I'm...uh, they call me King, said Fluffy.

Oh right! said Kiss. **I bet your name is really Binky, or Cutie, or Fluffy!**

How did she know? thought Fluffy.

I'm a crested guinea pig,
Kiss told Fluffy.
Crested guinea pigs are the best.

What are you doing in my yard?
Fluffy asked Kiss.
Anything I want, said Kiss,
who was bigger and fatter than Fluffy.
Uh . . . , said Fluffy. **Okay.**

I need a snack, said Kiss.

What have you got to eat?

Half of Fluffy's valentine apple

was in the play yard.

Fluffy hoped Kiss wouldn't see it.

But she did.

Kiss ran over to the apple.
She started chomping on it.
Fluffy ran over, too.
Grrrrr, growled Kiss. **Get away!**
It's my apple, said Fluffy.
Not anymore, said Kiss.
Fluffy watched Kiss eat his apple.
His bright red valentine apple.
It made him so mad!

What do you do for fun around here?
Kiss asked Fluffy.
I have some toys, Fluffy told her.
All I see is a bunch of junk, said Kiss.
Junk! said Fluffy. **Okay, Kiss,** he thought.
You asked for it!

You can climb in the cardboard box,
Fluffy told Kiss. **Or in the coconut shell.**
But don't go in the tube.
Why not? asked Kiss.
You wouldn't like it, said Fluffy.
I want to go in the tube, said Kiss.
Don't, said Fluffy. **I'm warning you.**
But Kiss scurried over to the tube.
Whatever you do, Fluffy called after her,
don't RUN into the tube!
Kiss started running.
She ran faster and faster.

She ran right into the tube.

Fluffy went around to the other side of the tube.

He poked his head in.

I...uh, I think I'm stuck, said Kiss.

Fluffy shook his head.

I tried to warn you, he said.

The Valentine's Day party ended.

Jemal and Emma came for the guinea pigs.

"Oh, no!" Emma said.

"Kiss is stuck in the tube!"

Jemal pulled on Kiss and she popped out.

Look at my crest! Kiss said.

Yeah, said Fluffy. **It's all messed up.**

Emma picked up Fluffy.

Jemal picked up Kiss.

“Do you think they fell in love?”

asked Emma.

“I don’t think so,” said Jemal.

I don’t think so either,

thought Fluffy.